CAPPUCINO THOUGHTS: COFFEE TIME CHIT CHAT

KSHAMA RAO

Made with ♥ on the Notion Press Platform
www.notionpress.com

I gratefully dedicate this book to the readers.

Contents

1. THE BEST TIME FOR CREATIVITY — 1

2. BREAKFAST — 3

3. ATTENTION SEEKING BEHAVIOUR — 4

4. BULLIES — 6

5. THE SHEDDING OF TEARS — 7

6. EMOTIONAL DETACHMENT — 8

7. FEW LINES ABOUT MAHATMA GANDHI — 10

8. GANESHA — 13

9. TOO MUCH CORTISOL — 14

10. GOOD FRIEND — 16

11. WHAT WOULD LIFE BE LIKE IF THERE WAS NO PAIN? — 17

12. HATERS GONNA HATE — 19

13. WHO ARE THE HIJRAS? — 20

14. HOW TO GET GLOWING SKIN NATURALLY — 23

15. HUGS — 25

16. THINGS THAT ARE ILLEGAL IN INDIA BUT NOBODY CARES — 26

17. THE BENEFITS OF GOING ON VACATIONS — 27

18. SHIVA — 28

19. LOVE YOUR KIDS — 29

20. WORSHIPPING THE PLANETS — 30

21. HOW TO SAVE MONEY — 33

22. SLEEPING WITH A MOBILE PHONE — 35

Contents

23. WHY WE SHOULD STOP COMPARING OURSELVES WITH OTHERS — 36

24. TULASI — 38

25. WHAT AFFECTS SELF-ESTEEM? — 40

26. YOU MAY NOT BE WASHING THESE BODY PARTS — 41

CHAPTER ONE

THE BEST TIME FOR CREATIVITY

Brahma muhurta, also known as Amrita vela, is the period between 4 and 6 in the morning, occurring one and a half hours before sunrise. It is considered an ideal time for yoga, meditation, prayers, creative pursuits, and studying. This time is significant for aligning with our circadian rhythm. During Brahma muhurta, the pineal gland secretes hormones at its peak levels, and the body's cortisol, often referred to as the 'alarm hormone,' is also released.

Waking up during Brahma Muhurta is said to be good for the lungs and overall long-term health. Rising at this time may help combat obesity and diabetes, accelerate healing, and slow down ageing. It also provides an opportunity to absorb ample Vitamin D from the early sunlight. Engaging in sun salutations and nature walks are beneficial activities. This time is also ideal for reflecting on one's parents and gurus. Moreover, waking up during Brahma Muhurta is believed to extend one's lifespan, boost immunity, balance pH levels, and improve the absorption of minerals and vitamins. However, it is advised to avoid eating or engaging in stressful activities during this period.

Ill persons, pregnant women, elderly persons, and children should not be pressurized to wake up at Brahma muhurta. We should not sleep after waking up at Brahma muhurta.

CHAPTER TWO

BREAKFAST

Breakfast is essential to start a day. Breakfast is to break the twelve-hour fast. If we don't have our breakfast, it will lead to overeating during lunchtime.

Oats and nuts are excellent breakfast choices. Nuts help in preventing diseases such as cancer and diabetes. Idli, dosa, and upma are also great options. Accompanying breakfast with a glass of milk is beneficial. It's advised to have a hearty breakfast like a king, a moderate lunch like a prince, and a light dinner like a pauper while being mindful to not overindulge in any single item.

Breakfast is crucial as it fuels our daily activities and replenishes our body's glucose levels. It aids in boosting metabolism and supplies essential vitamins, minerals, and nutrition. Eating breakfast helps curb cravings for unhealthy foods and enhances memory. Incorporating green tea and coconut water into our morning routine is beneficial; green tea is rich in antioxidants, while coconut water provides vital electrolytes. It is especially important that children do not skip breakfast.

CHAPTER THREE

ATTENTION SEEKING BEHAVIOUR

Seeking compliments or stirring controversy can be indicative of a desire for attention from others. This may stem from loneliness, low self-esteem, an effort to reclaim a sense of worth, or jealousy towards those who receive more attention. Such behavior could also be rooted in negative childhood experiences or past instances of bullying.

Many people become uncomfortable when others get their attention or become the centre of attraction. Such people try to draw attraction from others by using their appearance, by seductive behaviour or by any other dramatic behaviour. Such people usually take many selfies. They may dress to impress. Narcissists always look for attention. They keep swaggering about their achievements. Such people are usually unable to maintain meaningful relationships. They try to cause problems for others and try to play the victim. They profess to be busy or ill. They spend too much time on social media by posting their selfies even if they don't get likes or they might be partying all the time. Such people need counselling.

Attention-seeking behaviour can be detrimental as it may easily hurt our friends, risking the loss of valuable relationships. Being the centre of attention doesn't always equate to financial gain, rendering such attention futile. There's a risk of becoming addicted to this attention, craving it increasingly. Exclusion from group photographs might lead to feelings of neglect. This behaviour could foster an inflated ego, a desire to dominate, and an expectation of VIP treatment. Individuals may feign kindness to garner attention, all the while denying their attention-seeking tendencies.

CHAPTER FOUR

BULLIES

It's acceptable to disagree with others' feelings, but mocking, controlling, or manipulating them is not. If someone is bullying you, it's important to communicate that their behaviour is unacceptable and to make it clear that if it persists, you will end the friendship.

It is unacceptable for a friend to reveal personal confidences. Mimicking or making negative comments about someone in public is also not okay. Additionally, friends should not dictate who you can or cannot be friends with. If things do not go well even after explaining your feelings to the bullies, it is time you should end the relationship.

CHAPTER FIVE

THE SHEDDING OF TEARS

Crying is a natural emotion that heals our hearts. It makes us feel better by reducing our anger. It emotionally clears sadness and resolves grief.

Crying can elevate our mood and promote healing. It is beneficial to cry as it is crucial for our mental well-being. Tears can alleviate stress and enhance our spirits. They allow us to release and free our emotions. Crying detoxifies the body, soothes pain, aids in sleep, improves vision, expels toxins, and clears bacteria, providing a cooling effect.

Crying is good for both men and women. Some people may need solitude while crying.

EMOTIONAL DETACHMENT

Being attached does not necessarily equate to being in love, as love is free from attachments. Detachment often stems from a fear of attachments. Emotional detachment involves a disconnection from others. While detachment can be beneficial in preventing negative emotions, it also leads to challenges in maintaining personal relationships, a tendency to avoid others, and difficulties in expressing emotions. Those who are detached may lose interest in enjoyable activities and prefer solitude. Thus, detachment can have its drawbacks as well.

Individuals who solve others' problems may be perceived as strong, leading to being taken for granted and potentially hurt. Emotionally detached individuals might resort to humour in serious situations due to a lack of empathy. They tend to dislike clinginess, and often, many may not understand what is happening in their lives.

The symptoms suggest that these individuals may have experienced past abuse. It's important for them to connect with trustworthy individuals and receive support from others. Examining their attachment patterns and cultivating self-love are beneficial practices. Additionally, meditation can be a helpful tool for them.

CHAPTER SEVEN

FEW LINES ABOUT MAHATMA GANDHI

Mahatma Gandhi was born in Porbandar, Gujrat to Mohandas Karamchand Gandhi and his fourth wife Putlibai. He spent 21 years of his life in Africa.

At that time, there was a lot of skin colour discrimination. He was asked to sit on the floor and when he didn't agree he was beaten up. Gandhi Ji was not allowed to sit with the white on the same train.

Gandhiji told the truth about his life in his autobiography. According to him, his weakness was his shy nature in his childhood. Later, slowly he developed leadership qualities.

He acknowledged that he had begun consuming goat meat with his friend Sheikh and had also visited a brothel. He was coerced into visiting the brothel where the expenses had been prearranged. Nevertheless, he felt uneasy in the brothel and decided to leave. The insult from a woman there made him question his masculinity, yet he aspired to remain devoted to his wife. Gandhi Ji empathized with the anguish a woman endures when her husband frequents a brothel. He observed that a woman's tolerance is immense, enduring every transgression her husband commits, while a man is not held to the same standard. He noted the stark contrast in consequences for infidelity, where a woman's life is destroyed and she is forsaken by her husband.

Gandhi Ji had cultivated the habit of smoking and stealing. Later one day, Gandhiji realized his mistake, confessed his stealing to his father, and took a vow that he would never commit the mistake again.

His friends in London had convinced him that not eating meat would make him appear weak, so he began to include it in his diet. However, after learning about the advantages of vegetarianism and wishing not to disappoint his parents, he eventually stopped consuming meat.

Even though he didn't marry Kasturba to satisfy his lust, he admits that slowly he developed lust towards her and couldn't concentrate on his studies.

From his childhood, he was known for his honesty. He held a strong belief in God and led a life that was like an open book. He advocated for vegetarianism, fasting, and silence. He would often observe silence and fast for weeks. Although he was a lawyer, he lived a life of simplicity, akin to that of a poor person, and chose not to wear elaborate clothing. He crafted his own clothes using a spinning wheel. Gandhi Ji's diet was limited to vegetables, and he dressed in a single dhoti, embodying simplicity.

Gandhi Ji travelled the world to assist the impoverished and offered prayers to God. He was an advocate for non-violence. Despite being bestowed the title "Mahatma" by Rabindranath Tagore, Gandhi Ji humbly declined it. He was a prominent freedom fighter, leading the Swaraj and Satyagraha movements. Additionally, Gandhi Ji was an accomplished writer and was honoured with the title "Mahatma" by Rabindranath Tagore.

Mahatma Gandhi was assassinated by Nathuram Godse at Birla House in Delhi. Amidst a crowd, Godse bowed to Gandhi and fired three bullets into his chest and abdomen using an automatic pistol. As he succumbed, Gandhi was heard uttering "Ram! Ram!"

CHAPTER EIGHT

GANESHA

Ganapathi is the son of Lord Shiva and Lord Parvathi. He has a human body but an elephant face. The mouse is his vehicle. His favourite food is laddoo.

Ganesha, known as Vighnaharta, is revered for removing obstacles from our lives. He is also called Mangal Murti, signifying his role in eliminating adversity. Many keep his image in their homes as a symbol of good fortune. He is considered the deity of wisdom and is closely associated with Goddess Lakshmi. The form of Lakshmi Ganapathi is regarded as one of the most auspicious manifestations of Lord Ganesha.

Lord Ganesha helps his devotees from mischief makers. Lord Ganesha purifies our life. His pooja blesses us with good fortune and good health.

We should worship God out of devotion and not just to get accolades. Worshipping god and expecting something from him will not cause liberation. It will lead to our rebirth.

CHAPTER NINE

TOO MUCH CORTISOL

Excess fat around the midsection can be a sign of potential heart attack risk in the future. Elevated cortisol levels, often due to stress, are a primary cause of this fat accumulation. Stress may also lead to high cholesterol, headaches, digestive issues, menstrual irregularities, a sluggish metabolism, depression, and insomnia. During menopause, the body is prone to store fat centrally as the liver is nearby, which it perceives as beneficial. Consequently, rather than dieting, which can signal the body to conserve fat due to perceived scarcity, it is advisable to eat several small meals throughout the day and not skip breakfast.

To reduce midsection fat, we should begin our day with a glass of water, cook our meals at home, and ensure a restful night's sleep to maintain heart health.

Maintaining movement and flexibility in our bodies is essential. Simple activities such as walking or taking the stairs contribute to our health. Yoga, sports, and aerobic exercises are also advantageous. Engaging in sexual activity or dancing to music can be both pleasurable and a form of good exercise.

Consuming dark chocolate and nuts benefits heart health. Engaging in laughter and playful activities serves as an effective remedy. It's advisable to avoid bad fats and embrace good fats instead. Reducing salt consumption and enhancing fibre intake through fruits and vegetables is beneficial. Incorporating protein into every meal is essential. Maintaining a positive outlook on life, striving for happiness, and being free from anxiety are important. Adopting a pet can be advantageous. Regular blood tests are crucial for monitoring health.

CHAPTER TEN

GOOD FRIEND

A good friend is someone whose company you enjoy. You share similar interests and can engage in conversations and laughter together. They are always there for you, offering a shoulder to cry on. They respect your need for space yet provide support during difficult times. They value you, are trustworthy, and show understanding. They refrain from gossiping about you and remain neutral during your conflicts with others. They are responsive to your calls and avoid giving you the silent treatment.

They are like an open book; you're familiar with their quirks, and they're well-versed in your family dramas. They're willing to hang out and spend time with you. Cheerful and playful, they grasp your moods and are aware of your actions. They stand up for you and consistently strive to bring you joy. They don't compete with you; instead, they aim to inspire you.

CHAPTER ELEVEN

WHAT WOULD LIFE BE LIKE IF THERE WAS NO PAIN?

Happiness is not devoid of pain; it is an integral part of life. Evading pain only leads to greater suffering. In avoiding pain, we miss out on crucial life lessons. Thus, pain is necessary. Constant happiness is unattainable; we must acknowledge and address the negative aspects of life. The contrast between pain and happiness is essential. Pain is not detrimental; it helps us appreciate happiness more deeply.

If we become too cosy in life, our strength to endure hardship becomes compressed. Too much happiness causes unrealistic high self-esteem, excessive urges to talk, and even loneliness. Pain can enhance our social bonding; it can bring rewards and it teaches us to live in the present by accepting the situation. We should learn to handle happiness and sadness correctly. That is the beauty of our life and this life is a gift of God. They both are important and we cannot live without them.

CHAPTER TWELVE

HATERS GONNA HATE

Haters consider you as their enemy and not a friend. Some people never like you. They try to break you and devalue your accomplishments. Their behaviour will perturb you.

Such haters may be loners, egoistic, jealous, less successful, or different from you. They hate you if you are popular, loved, and getting attention. They hate you when you stand up for something. You may be having haters as you have a big circle of friends and all you have to do is to sort out your sincere friends and fake friends. Haters try to defame you and they even lie about you. They never like your social media posts.

You cannot change the hater's attitude. All you should do is set barriers and make new friends. You should not waste your energy on such people. You can take counselling if you are surrounded by many haters.

CHAPTER THIRTEEN

WHO ARE THE HIJRAS?

HIjras or Kinnars are also people but they come in between the male and female categories. You might have seen them demanding cash. Kinnars usually do not like their names as they refer to them as the opposite gender. They do not show interest in activities related to their gender. They have frustration over their genitals.

In India, it is believed that their blessings hold special and powerful significance. They are often invited to weddings and to places celebrating the birth of a child. Their curses are thought to bring numerous troubles in life. It is believed that they are blessed by Lord Shri Ram and endowed with the power to bless others. This is why people are afraid to upset them. Many Kinnars resort to using coarse language and inappropriate gestures to extort money from individuals, leaving people with the dilemma of choosing between giving money or facing a curse.

Aravan is their god. His marriage is enacted by the Kinnars and the next day they mourn his death and enact becoming widows. After this ritual, they are free to find a new partner. According to History, the Pandavas chose to sacrifice Arjuna's son Aryavanan for a good cause. The boy agreed but he wanted to marry before dying. No one was ready to get married their daughter to him and Lord Krishna faked the form of a beautiful Mohini and married him.

In Mahabharata, Shikhandi was a Kinnar. He had helped Arjuna to defeat Bhishma and Arjuna himself had disguised himself as a Kinnar for a year. According to History, Kinnars used to work as servants in palaces or used to work as guards. It is a belief that Yellamma wife of sage Jamadagni returned home late and he suspected her chastity. He ordered his five sons to cut her head. The first four sons didn't adhere to his order and his last son Parashurama decapitated her. Her head multiplied by tens and hundreds and moved to different regions. Her four sons turned into her followers. The Eunuchs believe that they are her sons. They also believe that they are cursed by Bahuchara Mata who was a princess in her last life and had cursed a man who tried to rape her to become sterile and freed him of the curse saying that he should act like a woman then only he can retain his potency. The eunuchs visit her temple and seek her blessings to get normal genitalia in their next birth. They believe that they are born as eunuchs because of their past life evildoings.

Eunuch Gurus are believed to possess special abilities, such as the power to see their own sins and those of others. Consequently, Kinnars often hold their gurus in high regard, sometimes even fearing them. These gurus are also thought to have the ability to predict death, a power attributed to those born as Eunuchs. In India, eunuchs who pass away are considered celestial beings and are often associated with having supernatural powers. Unlike the common practice, Hindu eunuchs are not buried; instead, they are taken to a secluded place upon death. There, they are given a ritual bath with Ganga water before being cremated, with their rituals performed in isolation.

CHAPTER FOURTEEN

HOW TO GET GLOWING SKIN NATURALLY

Inadequate sleep and pollution have made it incomplete for us to attain glowing skin. Here are some home remedies from the kitchen to attain glowing skin.

TURMERIC

Turmeric has antioxidant properties. It eradicates free radical damage to the skin and boosts collagen production. You can apply a paste of turmeric on your face and wash it after ten minutes.

HONEY

Honey moisturizes your skin. It dissolves blemishes and abates acne. It has bleaching properties. Apply it to your face and cleanse it with warm water after ten minutes.

ORANGE

Apply orange juice directly or apply a mix of orange peel powder and rose water on your face. Leave it for ten minutes and rinse with water.

MILK OR YOGURT

You can apply milk or yoghurt to your face. Allow it to dry

and then wash it with water.

BESAN

You can apply a Besan pack and wash it after leaving it on your face for ten minutes.

Other than these cucumber, lemon, Aloe Vera and papaya packs are good for the skin.

Always remove your makeup and apply these face packs. Certain medical conditions may also cause problems to the skin.

CHAPTER FIFTEEN

HUGS

Hugs make us gleeful. It can get rid of negative emotions and boost happy hormones in our bodies. Hugging is good for our heart health. It helps us get rid of lonesomeness. It helps in weight loss, increases our libido, lowers blood pressure, increases our immune system, and reduces stress. It is scientifically accepted that a mother's hug can lead to the total development of the baby. It increases bonding.

Hugging has anti-aging benefits, aids in treating insomnia, and soothes our muscles. It curbs food cravings by boosting Oxytocin levels in our body, which in turn reduces emotional eating. Additionally, hugging enhances our self-esteem, alleviates fears, elevates our mood, fosters empathy towards others, and enhances social interactions.

According to studies we need ten hugs a day for growth. It develops a feeling of positiveness. It makes us happy.

THINGS THAT ARE ILLEGAL IN INDIA BUT NOBODY CARES

Employing children below fourteen is illegal in India. But still, we can see children working on the roadside and in garages. Children are given birth just to juice money from them. Unlicensed sex rackets, prostitution, and exploitation are part of red-light areas. Many female children grow up as prostitutes. Girl child abortion is illicit in India but still, female fetuses are getting scraped off before birth. Begging mafias are all over the country.

Illegal liquor which is mixed with chemicals is sold in India and they are injurious to our health. Poor people consume this poison and succumb soon. Milk and food products like turmeric are contaminated in India.

CHAPTER SEVENTEEN

THE BENEFITS OF GOING ON VACATIONS

Taking a vacation can significantly reduce stress. It has been linked to a decreased risk of heart disease and can alleviate insomnia. Vacations can contribute to fitness, enhance brain function, and stabilize emotions. Additionally, they may help prevent diabetes by lowering cortisol production, improving digestion, and supporting healthy weight loss.

Going on vacations can improve our libido, strengthen our bones and enhance immunity. All this will lead to good sleep, more energy, and more happiness in life as our mind remains cool and our body gets detoxed. It can improve our hair quality, and skin quality, reducing migraine and chances of getting dementia. Going out on vacation can improve our memory and promote faster healing. It brings more opportunities for networking and making new friends. A shift is very crucial for us.

SHIVA

Lord Shiva is known for his simplicity, eschewing all adornments. He holds a deep affection for devotees who are virtuous and pure-hearted. He disciplines yet protects all creatures. His devotees receive his blessings, while the wicked face his punishment. He stands as the epitome of justice.

Lord Shiva is Adi Yogi. He confers us with peace. He is also Dakshinamoorthy who bestows the devotees with cognition. In the form of Kalabhairav and Veerabhadra, he crushes our adversaries.

Lord Shiva is depicted as sharing half of his body with Parvati. His sons are Ganesha and Kartikeya. He grants his devotees the blessing of a good family. Renowned as a magnificent dancer, he also endows his followers with wealth and fame.

Pleasing Shiva is very simple so he is also known as Bholenath. Shiva is also worshipped in the form of Linga. He loves animals and that is why he is known as Pashupathi. He consumed the poison which was discharged during Samundar Manthan, so he is called Neel Kant.

Visiting his temple on Monday, after 4 PM is very auspicious. You can wear a Rudraksha bead and it will give the same result of Shiva being with you.

LOVE YOUR KIDS

Children require ample love at home. It's beneficial to express appreciation for your spouse in the presence of your children to foster a sense of gratitude in them. Avoid casting blame on your spouse in front of the children. Should a conflict arise, address it in a manner that spares the children any distress.

You can look for ways to provide for the spouse. Give them gifts, give them surprises and go out with them or have a hobby with them. Try to spend quality time with them. Express love and affection. Be affectionate with them. Cook or buy his/her favourite meal. Celebrate their success and give them a massage often. Your children will become happy when you love and respect your spouse.

CHAPTER TWENTY

WORSHIPPING THE PLANETS

SUN

The sun governs our interactions and leadership, representing the paternal figure. To reduce disputes and conflicts within our home, it is advised to venerate Surya Dev. Offering water mixed with vermilion to the Sun God in a copper or brass vessel is customary, ensuring that both hands are raised above the head during the offering, and the water does not touch our feet. Adding rice to the water is also a practice, but plain water should never be offered. Chanting the Aditya Hridaya Stotra is believed to calm the Sun God. Donations of yellow or red fabric, jaggery, wheat, and red sandalwood are also said to please the deity. Chhath Puja is a festival dedicated to the Sun God.

MOON

The moon is believed to influence the balance of our hormones. It's beneficial to take a moonlit walk, gaze upon the moon, and meditate during the full moon. Worshipping Lakshmi on this day is said to bring prosperity. Performing the Satyanarayan Katha on Purnima is a common practice. It is also said that Krishna performed the Raas Leela on this night. Many deities, such as Subramanya, Dattatreya, and

Buddha, are revered for their birth on Purnima.

MARS

Worshipping Mars gives us vitality and courage.

MERCURY

Wednesday is the day of Lord Mercury. This day is also of Lord Krishna and Lord Ganesh. We should donate green vegetables and bangles on Wednesday.

JUPITER

Jupiter was born with eleven faces. He is said to be an embodiment of Lord Vishnu. Thursday is his day. Jupiter causes Gajakesari yoga, Hamsa yoga, and Pancha Mahapurush yoga in our horoscope. Jupiter is known for amplification. Becoming famous, gaining respect in society, and progressing are represented by Jupiter. He rules organs like the liver and lower abdomen. It expands everything it touches in astrology. It represents temples and colleges. Professions related to Jupiter are Pandit, lawyer, teacher, minister, banker, etc. It is a symbol of our past life's good actions. People with Jupiter in Lagna can become fat as Jupiter expands even the body size.

We should apply a turmeric tilak on Thursday and pray to Jupiter to please him. We should donate yellow clothes on Thursday. Fasting on this day is very favourable. Fasting without drinking water will resolve health ailments and ward off sins. A married woman should not wash their hair on Thursday. We should worship goddess Lakshmi also on this day to improve our finances. Offering yellow garland in the Vishnu temple will appease Lord Vishnu who controls Jupiter. Worshipping banana trees and donating Chana dal is beneficial.

VENUS

We should listen to Lalita Sahasranam and listen to Lord Parashurama's stories. We should listen to Ashtalakshmi's stotra and worship Goddess Lakshmi to please Venus. We should spend wisely to respect Venus. Doing creative activities also pleases Venus. We should be thankful for all our positive relationships. We should maintain hygiene and keep our homes clean. We should respect our spouse to strengthen Venus and bring a smile to the face of a woman who has struggled a lot in her life.

SATURN

Lord Saturn is revered for valuing donations. It is believed that we should give generously without anticipating reciprocation. Learning about Saturn's magnificence and venerating the Peepal tree are also suggested. To honour Saturn, it is recommended to walk barefoot on grass on Saturdays, worship Lord Hanuman, and conduct Yagyas. Discipline is emphasized, as is feeding the needy on Saturdays. It is advised to discard what hinders our advancement and to engage in selfless service, sharing in the collective hardships to appease Saturn.

CHAPTER TWENTY-ONE

HOW TO SAVE MONEY

Our daily expenses include household bills, rent, food, sanitation products, entertainment, etc. Our irregular expenses include clothing, travelling, medication, etc.

Purchasing in bulk, as well as preparing and packing our own lunches, can lead to significant savings. This practice reduces the amount spent on restaurant meals. It's advisable to limit online shopping. Changing our mobile phone plans can also aid in budget management. Being inventive with gifts is another cost-effective strategy. Additionally, we can lower our expenses by reducing electricity and gas consumption. It's essential to monitor our savings and spending closely.

Reselling old items is a viable option. Instead of watching TV, we can opt for internet plans to stream on mobile devices. Collectively pooling funds with neighbours for gifts, dining out, and internet packages can be advantageous. Hosting house parties rather than going out to restaurants, and attending open festivals and events over private parties can also lead to savings. Additionally, creating DIY beauty and hygiene products can contribute to cost-cutting. These methods can effectively help in saving money.

CHAPTER TWENTY-TWO

SLEEPING WITH A MOBILE PHONE

Sleeping with a mobile near our head will cause sleep deprivation and will alter the quantity and quality of sleep. You may get a headache the next day morning due to screen exposure and electromagnetic radiation. The blue spectrum light discharged from the mobile makes our brain think that it is daytime. The night mode however will decrease this effect. It decreases the Melatonin levels in our body. It resets our circadian rhythm and alters hormones in our body and affects our metabolism, blood sugar, and immunity. Watching movies, reading, or playing games on the screen before going to sleep is a bad habit. We can use earbuds or Bluetooth speakers to listen to music.

Chances are there that the phone may even burst if we charge it overnight. It is necessary to remove our phones from the bedroom and keep an alarm clock to wake us up in the morning. We can put our mobile into night mode or aeroplane mode.

CHAPTER TWENTY-THREE

WHY WE SHOULD STOP COMPARING OURSELVES WITH OTHERS

Comparing ourselves with others damages our sense of self. We may feel less fortuitous and become jealous of others. It doesn't help in accomplishing our goals.

We all compare ourselves with others and it is not easy to stop doing so. We should understand that we all have different roadways. We all are different in a way and are accomplished in different ways. There will always be someone better than us in some activities.

Life is not always fair; some people will be having more advantages than us like they can be rich and so on. When we stop comparing ourselves with others, there will be nothing to fear and we can become more gifted. This is why we should stop comparing ourselves and making ourselves feel bad. We should not become envious of our friends but become glad of them.

CHAPTER TWENTY-FOUR

TULASI

Tulasi is a green plant. She is the beloved of Lord Krishna. She was an admirer of Krishna and Krishna had killed her husband, a demon named Jalandhara, who had gotten strength from her purity. Lord Shiva couldn't defeat Jalandhara in a war, because of Tulsi's purity. At this time, Lord Vishnu takes the form of Jalandhara and Tulsi welcomes him thinking that he is her husband. Only because of this greeting, does her modesty get destroyed as she believed Vishnu to be Jalandhara. Taking this opportunity, the demigods kill Jalandhara. After knowing the truth, Tulasi curses Lord Vishnu to become a stone. Lord Vishnu accepted her curse and became Saligrama in the Gandaki river and granted her the position of his spouse in Vaikunta. He never accepts any food without Tulasi and even Lakshmi sometimes gets envious of Tulsi.

Tulasi and Vrinda are the same. She is an evolution of Radha Rani. Vrinda Devi controls Vrindavana.

We should water Tulasi and circumnutate her three times in the morning. We should never cut or prune the Tulsi plant and we should immediately dispose of the plant if it dies. Before offering anything to Krishna, we should first offer him Tulsi leaves. We should not cook Tulsi and consume it in the form of tea; it is a sin. We should pray to her with great faith and offer her incense sticks and ghee Diya in the evening. Before spunking the leaves, we should ask for her forgiveness and take permission that we are offering her to Krishna. We should not sprinkle chemicals on her.

Tulsi purifies our houses. One who worships Lord Krishna with Tulsi will attain liberation.

CHAPTER TWENTY-FIVE

WHAT AFFECTS SELF-ESTEEM?

An unhappy relationship, losing our loved ones, or serious illness can lower our self-esteem. Stressful experiences, an unhappy childhood, and downfalls in life may also diminish our self-esteem. As per research, our self-esteem will be low in childhood, maximum in adulthood, and again low in old age.

We should convert negative events into positive ones to boost our self-esteem in life. We should take care of ourselves and do things that we appreciate. We should spend time with people who make us happy and also stop comparing ourselves with others. We should be active and try to look our best. We must identify ourselves in life and welcome life as it is and work more on our strengths. We should have a target in life.

YOU MAY NOT BE WASHING THESE BODY PARTS

You may not be cleaning a few of your body parts.

Do you wash behind your ears? The sebum gets clustered behind your ears and it may become foul-smelling. You may not be brushing your fingernails. The culture of bacteria is very high in your belly button. The bacteria may even cause a bad smell.

People usually clean their hair but forget to clean their scalps. The scalp contains many sweat and oil glands. It may cause dandruff. So, you must stroke your scalp while washing.

Do you clean the space between your toes? Dirt and bacteria build-up takes place there. You should wash this area and dust the talcum powder regularly. Your tongue is the breeding area for bacteria. You should scrape your tongue regularly.

Do you clean under your breasts? Residue builds up in this area and may cause itching. You should clean your back with a scrubber. It will flake off the dead skin and give you healthier skin.

You should also focus on the back of your neck. You should even check if you are overlooking your elbow and creases. Take care to wash the sides and bottom of your feet. Germs can grow in your private parts and cause irritation or odour.